The new neighbors have
arrived. Look, a girl
is waving at Kim!

Kim, Carrots, Mommy, and Daddy walk
over to say hello. They bring cookies.

Kim says hello to Mia, and Carrots
says hello to Mia's puppy, Buzz.

While Mommy and Daddy
help carry boxes . . .

Kim and Mia play together.
It's fun to make new friends!

Morning Verse

Anonymous
Art by Karen Dugan

 Down is the earth,

 Up is the sky,

 There are my friends,

 And here am I.

 Good morning, good morning.

Piano Play

by Kathleen Bahr ✱ Art by Marci Chorpash

Plink-a-plink! Plink-a-plink!
I play my favorite song.
Plink-a-plink! Plink-a-plink!
Will you sing along?

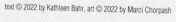

Grandma's Coming

by Elizabeth Steinglass ✳ Art by Viviana Garofoli

Red cars, blue cars, black cars, gray,
pass our house and zoom away.
Look! A pink car's coming near.
No more waiting! Grandma's here!

Look around you. Do you see any colors from the poem?

Winter Cuddles

by Sarah Meade
Art by Heegyum Kim

snow shimmers
ice glimmers
pretty winter weather

quilt cuddles
warm snuggles
reading books together

Den O

A Mother Goose Rhyme
Art by Jo Brown

John ran up to the top of the hill
And blew his whistle loud and shrill.
Said the fox, That is very pretty music. Still⁓

g

Follow me
to the
Guide for
Caregivers!

So Many Cuddles

by Dennis R. Brown

Have you had a cuddle today? It might have been . . .

a warm bear hug, a greeting for a friend,